The Last Dance

By Colin Bass

Corinthians 4:18

"While we look not at the things which are seen, but at the things which are not seen: for the things which are seen are temporal; but the things which are not seen are eternal.

This book is not a true story, but simply a story to evoke thought. A story about the love shared between a parent and a child, and how easily that bond can be broken and repaired. As a parent you have a responsibility to your offspring to love, cherish, and make them as happy as possible. Remember parenting is not a job; it is a gift a blessing bestowed upon you by God. So love every moment, and any chance you get tell your children you love them. Tell your children how special they are, because a child can never receive too much praise.

Prologue

After ten hours of patiently waiting you entered the world. I would be your father, and she would be your mother. You were 6 lbs. 8oz. of beauty, one of God's most incredible creations, but best of all you were ours. You were given to us to take care of, and I failed you. I failed you miserably, and for that I am sorry. I wish I could go back and rewrite my wrongs, rewrite the past, but in the end I must live with the guilt, the guilt of not being all that you deserved.

I stared into your eyes, and made a silent promise as your father. I promised that I would always care for you, keep you free of harm, and be there when you needed me most. I fell short, and I issue a thousand apologies but I know the man I have become is too proud to admit this fact.

I ask for time, but that is an abstract concept. Webster defines time as, *the indefinite continued progress of existence and events in the past, present, and future regarded as a whole*. I on the other hand define time as something people like to waste.

"All you have is time," people say or one of my personal favorites "Just give it time and you will see." See what? What happens when all this time people speak of runs out? What happens when death is staring us right in the face can we look at him and say, "can't you just give me a little more time?"

I have wasted my time with everything, but I never dedicated my days to being the father that would guide you through the torrential terrain of life. I just hope that one day you will be able to look me in the eyes and accept the two words I have desperately longed to say, I'm sorry.

II Corinthians: 12:9

"…My grace is sufficient for thee: For my strength is made perfect in weakness."

Chapter 1: Reminiscing

You don't know what it's truly like to feel pain until your child looks at you and asks, "Who are you?" I guess twenty-three years of absentee fatherhood has caught up with me.

So here I sit with a glass of whiskey in one hand, and my ticket to the afterlife in the other. I guess it's my fault. I'm unmarried with one child, Gabrielle, who has just turned 35. She is married with kids of her own who don't know I exist.

Self-pity was never a characteristic I possessed, but all it took was that one day about twelve years ago when I went to my daughter's graduation.

I've always kept in contact with my daughter's mother, I guess if you call the occasional letter contact, but never with my daughter. Being an alcoholic tollbooth operator isn't exactly something you want to share with some who spends their adolescence idolizing you.

So I kept my distance feeling ashamed, and scared. I was around for the first 11 years of her life, but my drinking became too much, and my ex-wife left me taking Gabrielle with her.

I have held a myriad of jobs; my best was being an attorney for one of the largest law firms in Chicago. Oh how the mighty have fallen. So I now sit here with a half empty glass of whiskey and a cold loaded pistol in the other hand. The pistol, frigid, lifeless, but with one simple pull of the trigger it can say so much.

I recall twenty-three years ago when I attended my daughter's graduation from one of the most prestigious universities in America. She is so smart, graduated at the top of her class, and was so involved. Law Schools were drooling over her after graduation. I would like to say she gets it from me, but examining the state of my life it appears as if that is far from the truth. I used to be a man of worth, with self-confidence, and the type of person people enjoyed to have in their company. But now I am sad, directionless and a figurative black hole anyone that gets close to me has their hopes and dreams stripped away from them.

The day of her graduation Gabrielle looked gorgeous, those dark curls falling to her shoulders, those beautiful big brown eyes, and her lovely almond colored skin. Looking at her was like living a dream. I couldn't have been more proud.

I stood at the back of the gymnasium and watched them call the graduates up one by one. When they got to Gabrielle it took all I had not to scream with excitement.

Instead I sobbed. Luckily the kind woman standing near me handed me a hanker chief. After each graduate was given the chance to stroll across the stage, and enjoy the applause from their loved ones, they were asked to stand one last time. The crowd congratulated them with a roar of cheers followed by more applause. They then proceeded to throw their caps in the air. During the commotion my eyes never left Gabrielle. My gaze was fixated upon my loving daughter, and I wondered if given the chance to speak with her what I would say? Would she know me? Would she hate me?

I waited impatiently until the ceremony was over. I stood silently as I watched Gabrielle hug and kiss friends and family.

She was then alone, and I knew this was my chance. A present tucked neatly under my arm, a wind up carousel that played "you are my sunshine," her favorite song when she was a child. I approached her slowly and meticulously. When we met eyes all she said was "Do I know you?" She gave me a look that froze time, and I began to feel unsure. I felt like I had made a mistake. I wanted to turn and run, but instead I attempted to speak. All I could muster was "I… I… I…" She gave me a knowing look, but what came out next was harder to take than a bullet.

She frowned, "Who are you?" she said. The words stuck in the air like stale cigarette smoke, and in that moment all my mistakes came back to bite me in the ass. I will never know if she meant it but it hurt none-the-less. The next sentence that left my mouth was coated in sadness, "congratulations miss." We haven't spoken since.

I guess this is why I sit here wallowing in self-pity. I have watched life pass me by, but I refuse to let it go on. Whiskey untouched since the last sip. Pistol still loaded, and ready for its last go. Face and shirt soaked with tears. I have a letter written to Gabby, who else needs to know why I have grown weary in life? I ask myself is this it? Is this what life has become? I can think of a million reasons to die, but only one to live. Still that one reason isn't enough. So I cry my last tears, and hear the faint words of Eric Clapton's Tears In Heaven playing in the background.

If I ever see Gabby in heaven will she know me? She probably wouldn't speak two words to me the way I have treated her. I guess I couldn't really blame her. And with that fleeting thought I sigh, my last of many sighs.

Psalms 118:1

"O give thanks unto the Lord; for he is good: Because his mercy endures forever."

Chapter 2: Downward Spiral

I remember. God do I remember. I woke up Jake Stevens attorney and ended the day as the man who had lost everything. I began that day the same as I did all others. I woke up and kissed my beautiful wife good morning. Danielle how could you leave me when I needed you most? You lost patience, but when? Was it the uncontrollable drinking? Was it my constant comatose state? I was stupid. It was all of it who am I kidding? How couldn't I see what I was doing to you and Gabby?

After kissing my wife I headed to the bathroom. I opened the top drawer just beneath my sink. I reached for the contents that I knew all too well and took my first shot of whiskey. It always burned, but the strong flavor would sweep deliciously across my taste buds. I did this each morning as if to say, "good morning old friend today is going to be a good day!"

I then got my daughter ready for school while Danielle cooked breakfast. The smell of bacon, eggs and coffee filled the house. I am hungry just thinking of it.

After getting Gabby ready I should have gotten prepared for work, but like the many days before and every other day this week I decided it would be best to stay home. Or should I say I took time off to do some much

needed drinking. It's just my hands don't feel right
without a drink and a cigarette (a bad habit I have had
since college, but Danielle has loved me, or did love me
regardless). I remember watching Danielle leave with Gabby
to take her to school. Danielle examined me in my bathrobe
and slippers, and I examined her in her black pantsuit that
seemed so ordinary, but she made look so gorgeous. Her
beautiful green eyes, her long brown hair, her gorgeous
lips, I could have stared at her for hours wondering how
God had blessed the world with something so perfect. Before
stepping out of the door Danielle asked me if I was finally
going to work, and I told her I had a late meeting so I
still had some time but I would. Lying to Danny was always
hard, but over the years it had become as easy as
breathing.

I then turned back and headed to my study. Tucked
behind the law books on my shelf was a brand new bottle of
the finest whiskey. I poured myself a drink, and one drink
shortly became two, and two became four, and four became
the whole bottle. Here is where my problem begins to show
itself, because the one bottle was never enough.

So I stumbled out of my study still wearing my
bathrobe and slippers. I then grabbed my keys by the door
that leads to the garage. I hopped into my car and drove to

the supermarket. "Two more bottles Jake?" I asked myself aloud "Why certainly" I responded. I stumbled around the aisles of the supermarket until I found the Holy Grail that I had been looking for, the liquor section. Each bottle spoke to me, as if saying "Drink me Jake, Drink me!" I obliged. Buying two of the most expensive bottles of my drink of choice. I might be an alcoholic, but I would never cheat my palate with something that belongs in the well.

After buying the two bottles of my liquid vice I stumbled out of the store, and back to my car. The funny part about all of this was that I had entered the store without closing my car door or shutting off the engine. So there sat my Mercedes door ajar, and still running waiting for the madness that was to ensue in my life.

I sat down in the drivers seat, and just as I began to shift into gear, my phone rang. I fumbled around a bit, and I found my phone in my bathrobe pocket. I answered with slurred speech. The call was from Gabrielle's school saying she had gotten into trouble, and they couldn't reach my wife at work and I needed to come immediately. My plans had changed so instead of drinking my afternoon away I had to pretend to be sober.

There I was on my way to Gabby's school, drunk at 12:00 in the afternoon. I arrived at the sanctuary that molded the minds of our youth DUI free miraculously, and still dressed for a day of drinking in the comfort of my own home.

I drunkenly traveled through the halls of my child's school, and I arrive in Gabrielle's empty classroom. The students were out for their period of lunch and recess, and there sat Gabrielle's teacher Miss Timkin. Every father's fantasy, drunk, and alone with a gorgeous young teacher. A fair toned woman, around the age of 26, about 5'7 with the legs of a… of a… well with great legs. Auburn colored hair, beautiful green eyes. In short she was one gorgeous young lady, and I had to control myself in my drunken haze not to jump all over her.

Miss Timkin asked me to sit down, and I did as I was told. On my way to the undersized seat in the front of the classroom I tripped on my own two feet. I quickly looked at Miss Timkin to see if she had noticed, but luckily her head was down as she was too busy shuffling papers. What are you looking for I wondered while I took my seat.

At this particular point sobriety was long gone, and there was nothing left but slurred speech and blurred vision. I was probably, actually I was certainly too drunk to focus on any kind of conversation especially one of this magnitude. The half a bottle of whiskey I downed in the car prior to entering the building was definitely catching up to me at this point.

Miss Timkin pulled a piece of paper off of her desk. It was a drawing.

I said "Oh how nice, did Grabby drew that?"

Miss Timkin turned her head, frowned, and squinted her eyes a bit as if to say are you all right? She then responded in a condescending tone "Is it nice? And yes Gabby did draw this. Mr. Stevens look at the bottom here."

I struggled with blurred vision, so the only thing I could make out was the drawing. It was a family portrait. We all looked happy so I couldn't figure out why it was so urgent for her to speak with me? I told Miss Timkin it was useless to have me try and read it, because I was not wearing my glasses. At this juncture Miss Timkin had gotten frustrated and made her way around her desk and was sitting on it with her legs crossed. My mind began to race as any mans would have. I began to think what it would be like to have the chance to navigate   …

She broke my train of thought. I had to direct my eyes upward so I would be looking her in the eye.

Miss Timkin began speaking impatiently. "Mr. Stevens"

"Please call me Jake" I responded.

"Okay! Jake. Gabby has been making these drawings, and writing on the bottom of these family portraits she so frequently draws. Since Gabby is only in the 4th grade I encourage self-expression, and writing whenever the moment strikes them, but this is absurd. I warned her the first time it happened, but now I had to call someone in. She has written white + nigger = Gabby. Now Mr. Stevens I understand that you are, um African American."

"Black, please" I responded. My timing for speech was not impeccable for she looked like a woman on a mission.

Miss Timkin went on, "I understand you are black, but where is she getting this outrageous mathematical equation."

I began to laugh, but the stern look upon the young teachers face was not one of a person entertained.

"Miss Timkin… Miss Timkin, Miss Timkin it's not rocket science, when someone such as myself, a negro if you will and someone like my wife, a white, get together and make a baby it makes a Gabby. Now I understand that you don't quite get this due to what I believe to be a um-racist background you posses, but I believe that all is fair in love and war and we should appreciate what we've got."

At that point I could tell Miss Timkin was not amused, she spoke timidly but stern. "Mr. Stevens I didn't want to jump to any conclusions, but are you," she paused momentarily trying to compose herself. "Well you seem to be drunk? I think you should go, and I will call Mrs. Stevens to handle this because it is obvious you are not fit to take on the problem."

Here is where I miss spoke, miss acted, just plain miss everythinged. I stumbled out of my undersized chair, and stood up the best I could. I placed my right hand upon the thigh of Miss Timkin, which may I add was everything I thought it was going to be.

I placed my hand on her thigh, and told her we didn't have to tell anyone and that we could do things that could just be our secret. After that I only remember waking up in the nurses office.

As my eyes adjusted to the florescent lighting I realized I was strewn out on a cot. I turned to my left where I saw a lonely looking old lady who seemed to be weathered by the winds of time, and I turned to my right and saw a woman. A young woman, a young woman with an angry face and I knew that face could only have belonged to Danielle Nicole Stevens. "Are you too drunk to drive?" she said this with pursed lips, one eyebrow raised, and a look of pure disgust on her face.

I spoke quietly "No."

She leaned in close to my ear, which sent cold chills down my spine as if I had just been told of a death in the family. She whispered "I know what you did to her, and we will fucking talk about this when you get home. Oh, and you should probably expect not to stay at the house tonight!"

After Danny stormed out I turned and asked the nurse what had happened. She told me I had slipped and knocked myself unconscious in Miss Timkin's room while I was there for a meeting. Later I realized that she punched my lights out after making a rude pass at her.

So when I arrived home after two bars, three bottles of whiskey, and 4 or 5 packs of cigarettes, a dark house greeted me. I hit the garage door opener, and watched the door opened never really paying attention to the fact that Danny's car was gone.

Proud of myself for managing to make it home safely, I stumbled into the house. I made sure to grab the bottle of whiskey from the toolbox in the garage for a celebratory drink. I never stopped to think that I should take the keys out of the ignition or more importantly shut the car off. I made my way to the living room, tripped over the coffee table, which I assume is the reason for the bruise I woke up with on my shin, and passed out on the floor.

I awoke to the sunlight piercing through the bay window in our living room, and not only that I awoke to the smell of vomit. As I searched for the reason for this putrid smell I realized I had slept in yesterday's meals. After examining the vomit, I went to the kitchen to find some cleaning supplies. I opened the cabinet by the refrigerator, but instead of reaching for the items to rid the house of the horrid smell, I grabbed my trusty bottle of kitchen whiskey and my hangover sunglasses tucked behind the bottle. I put the sunglasses on, and took a good morning chug of that fine, fine whiskey. A hangover was only a minor obstacle when it came to drinking, and I was sure I could drink my way out of the worst of them.

I set the bottle down and looked to the right near the refrigerator, and saw a note labeled "Jake." Before I picked up the letter I toweled off some of the vomit still clinging to my face and hands. I then thumbed the letter for a second wondering what it could possibly be. Danny's handwriting yes, but what did she have to write that she couldn't say to me in person? I opened it slowly, I could tell from the wrinkles on the letter that it was tear stained, and judging by some of the holes in the paper it was written in anger. I began to read:

Jake-

*I'm tired... Sick of it... Lonely... Where is my
husband? Where is my best friend? Where is the man I
fell in love with in college? The alcohol has taken
you away from me. The cigarettes I could handle, the
occasional drink I could handle, but this missing work
to go on 24hr drinking binges is all I can take. You
drove me to this. I still love you. I always will, but
I have to go.*

*Gabrielle and I have gone to my parents I will be
in touch, because I want, no I NEED time. You don't
look at me or touch me anymore. You are not my
husband, and I sure as hell don't know who you have
become. I wish it could be different, but it's not. If
you can promise to go to counseling, AA, start going
to work, and try to help fix us there may be a
relationship to salvage. It's up to you what happens
from here, but if you don't change I will know your
answer.*

Danny

P.S. What were you thinking when you hit on Miss Timkin? Our daughter's teacher? Jake that's even low for you.

Tears uncontrollably streamed from my eyes. I couldn't find the will to stop them. How could I live without Gabby and Danny? Who would I turn to? She says I need to change, but am I strong enough? I didn't talk to my family. What would I do? How would I cope? The Maker. He always knew what to do. How to calm me. How to take me somewhere new. Somewhere far away from this hell I was living.

I got up and started for the kitchen to find a bottle of whiskey. The phone began to ring, and I grabbed it thinking, hoping, and praying it was Danny. I picked it up, "Danny?" A man's voice greeted me from the other end, but not any man it was my boss. The lead partner at the firm I worked for, James Tomlin. His tone was somber, apologetic in a way.

I asked him what I could do for him.

"Are you coming in to work today Jake?"

Work? Oh my God work, I had completely forgotten. What day is it I thought? Oh shit Thursday! I played it cool, and told him I would more than likely take the day off.

"I'm sorry Jake, but it has been weeks since you have come into work, and I am beginning to wonder if you are a good fit for this firm. I know you are a hard worker, and you have a good heart but you have lost your way."

He was right, I hadn't been to work in weeks and when I did go I smelled like alcohol, the scent perforated from my pores like newly applied cologne, and I would still be wearing the same clothes from the day before.

Mr. Tomlin went on, "What has happened to you Jake? Why is it like this? What are you doing with yourself?"

I remained silent hoping that by not saying a word somehow he would understand how sorry I was. Mr. Tomlin was like a father to me, and a mentor that helped my law career blossom and transform into something special.

All I could do was weep for the life I once had. The tears were endless, the pain was extraordinary, and for the first time I contemplated suicide. I tried to listen to Mr. Tomlin speak, but unfortunately his words were falling on deaf ears.

He dealt me the final blow when he said, "I'm sorry Jake, but we have to let you go." I dropped the phone, and collapsed to my knees. Who am I? Where did I go wrong? Danielle come back to me.

I remember how your eyes, those beautiful green eyes used to fill my heart with butterflies. I used to count the wrinkles on your face when you smiled. I used to run my fingers through your long brown hair, and I was jealous that each strand was closer to you than I was. I wanted to be with you always. Oh my God what happened? I'm sorry, so sorry.

After the phone call I cried and drank for two days, I drank for a week, and I then drank for twenty-four years.

Danielle moved on and married, Gabrielle grew up, and Danielle sent the occasional photo. They say you never know what you've got until it's gone. It's true. Time stands still for no one I am a testament to that and a thousand other clichés. I am dead inside. A daughter who doesn't know me, an ex-wife who once loved me more than life itself. Maybe I should pray? But with a soul as lost as mine prayer is pointless. So here I sit, whiskey in my left hand, a friend that has always stood by me. A cigarette in my mouth, which I light with an unpaid bill. I look around my apartment everything covered in random paperwork, eviction notices, and letters I had once written to Danielle and Gabby. I never possessed the strength to send any of them, and I guess that is why I sit here alone. As I cry I wonder how many tears of self-pity I let drip from my

eyes over the years. Parents who have died and I didn't
attend their funerals. A brother and a sister with kids of
their own whom I have never met, nor really cared to meet.

A daughter who I don't know, with a husband and kids
of her own. I've only seen pictures, but the kids are
beautiful. I wish I could tell them they take after their
mother. I'm certain they are smart, and will grow up to do
great things.

I look to my ticket sitting on the end table and close
my eyes as I run my fingers across the cold steel. I cry as
I do this knowing that this will be the last of many things
I have touched. I have known the love of a good woman, the
happiness of parenting, and the sting of disappointment.
All things I will always remember. Is there something after
this? Is there a God? What will he or she say to me?

"I know I was bad," I will say. "I should go to hell
for being a man of little worth and no heart."

Will he take pity on me? Will she be forgiving? Is God
a man or woman? Questions that will be answered soon
enough.

I put the glass of whiskey to my lips, take a drink
and blow out the smoke still filling my lungs. If only
Danny and Gabby were still here. What would life be like?
But I was a bad husband and an even worse father. I take

another sip of whiskey, and another drag from my cigarette.
I put the glass to my lips again, and go to take a drink
but it's empty. I look to the bottle in my lap this too is
empty. I set it at my feet. I put my cigarette out in the
ashtray. I glance around a dimly lit apartment. The only
light that shines in the room I sit are the beams delivered
by the fading sun. I wipe away the last of many tears, and
pick up the last thing I will ever feel. My chair feels
more comfortable now. My hand trembles with the weight of
the pistol, and now I realize the tears that sat patiently
in the corners of my eyes are now taking their final
resting place upon my shirt.

"I love you Gabby and Danny." My last words spoken out
loud, but no one will hear them. I press the pistol to my
temple. And I pull the trigger. Hot. God what did I do? It
hurts, but only for a moment. And everything fades.

Psalms 118:5-9

"I called upon the Lord in distress: The Lord answered me, and set me in a large place. The Lord is on my side; I will not fear…"

Chapter 3: Memories

"Get up…Get up…" A voice I hear but whom does it belong to?

"Get up Daddy! Get up!" I open my eyes, and it's my daughter, Gabrielle. She's talking to me, but I'm not me. I am now watching me with her, my beautiful daughter. She is about 5 no she is 5. She is missing her front teeth, and I can remember how excited she was because this day was Christmas. Christmas of 1982.

I hear myself say to her "I'm up, I'm up."

She retorts with "Santa came Daddy. He ate the cookies and he left presents! Lots and lots of presents!" She bolts out of the room, back to all that makes Christmas beautiful to a child.

I see the blankets move, and a head rest on my chest. It's Danny, as beautiful as ever, her long brown hair, those stunning green eyes, and that soft melodic voice that could bring an angel to tears. We rise from bed, and go to see the commotion downstairs.

Gabby had already begun to open gifts. Some of which didn't even belong to her. Wrapping paper all over the place. Toys littered the floor. Gabby turned as we came down the stairs, and those big beautiful brown eyes were full of life and excitement.

I watched as Danny and I sat on the couch and looked on as Gabby mimicked a tornado jumping from one toy to another. Danny and I slowly unwrapped our gifts. I patiently waited for her to reach for the present I had worked so hard on.

I recall careful planning for weeks. The engagement ring I had bought her fresh out of college was small and slightly unattractive, a white gold band, and a diamond so tiny the pettiest of thieves wouldn't have taken it. Danny always said she loved it, and never complained about the size of the ring. Her carefree attitude was one of the reasons why I fell so deeply and desperately in love with her.

What happened? Why did I ruin things? When did I lose myself? When did I lose Gabby? When did I lose my family? Sickening to think that the man I had become was the man Danny didn't want.

Danny always took her ring off to shower so I seized my opportunity. I took the sign of my affection, and brought it to the best jeweler in Chicago, Malcolm Little. Malcolm was a jeweler with the vision of a genius. A tall man who said little but his work said so much. He took Danny's ring, and redid the setting. He put three one carat diamonds on the ring, and an inscription inside I can

proudly say were my words, and came straight from my heart.
It read, "Forever mine, we will never part." Oh how I was
wrong. I am the only one to blame.

The three diamonds were to signify Danny, Gabby, and
I. As Gabby gushed, and squealed with excitement, Danny
picked up the present I was sure would put me in the
Husband Hall-of-Fame. Danny who had been sad, almost to the
point I couldn't console her, unwrapped the reason for her
misery. See she thought by losing the ring her love for me
wasn't as strong as my love for her, something that was not
true. It took all I had not to tell her what happened.

She slowly undid the bow, and then turned to me with a
look of curiosity. "You didn't," she said as she thumbed
the box. She opened it, and tears began to fall from her
gorgeous eyes. And the smile I had searched for, and had
gone weeks without was back.

Gabby's laughter stopped, and she turned to her mommy
and asked if she was okay. The concern Gabby showed was
that of someone beyond her years. Danny kissed me over and
over. Sobbed, and continuously told me she loved me.

Danny picked up the ring, and I told her to read the
inscription. I thought at this point her tears had reached
the end, but more fell from her eyes. I slid the ring on
her finger. She asked me why I hadn't told her? Why did I

let her cry? I told her it was because I loved her and I had always wanted to do this. She smiled, and all 26 of her wrinkles showed up on her face. I kissed away her tears, and at the point I couldn't have loved her more. My two women were happy, and I couldn't have asked for a better Christmas present.

I stand there in awe trying to figure out how I could be watching a memory that belongs to me? But before I can lose myself in thought everything goes black. Where am I? Am I dead? Am I me? A voice I have never heard says to me "yes, you are dead." It proceeds to tell me how I died. It is a man's voice, strong, and I feel as if I can trust him. He speaks to me with sincerity. He says to me "you're okay now, you're home."

"Home? Where is home?" I say. Lights turn on and I am sitting next to a man in a place that is so familiar.

He turns to me and asks if I remember the building we are sitting in?

I think… I don't know it looks… it feels… He cuts off my thoughts as if I am thinking aloud.

"Buckeye Theater."

I think, think, and I remember the theater I use to take Gabrielle to every Thursday for dollar movies. I break, and I begin to cry.

The man just waits, he gives a comforting silence. A man no older than I, with slightly graying hair, and a clean-shaven look. Handsome, but in the classical sense. He touches my shoulder and says, "everything is okay you're home now."

I think home? Why does he keep saying home? He responds as if I am speaking. "Heaven of course."

I turn to him and ask "why me? I was a horrible person, father, husband, son, and brother! I was shit, and I should go to hell."

He only smiles as if to say no, no you were none of those. He opens his mouth, and what he says next was more devastating than Danny leaving me. "Your daughter misses you, and since you have killed yourself she is beating herself up for not trying harder to see you. She loves you Jake."

I look at him curious. I dare not question what he says so I remain silent. I want to inquire what he means, but the thought of Gabby upset with my departure is almost too much for me to bear.

He tells me he is my guardian angel, and he has always been watching over me. He tells me his name, James. The name rings in my head like bells on New Years Eve.

"James?" I say as if trying to stir up an old memory.

He says "like your twin brother that was lost during birth."

I examine his face, and it's so much like mine. I cry, and I ask "Why? Why have you dedicated your existence to me?"

He only smiles and puts his head down. He then looks at me with tears in his eyes. "It's because I love you, brother." I go to say something, but he only takes the words out of my mouth. "I know I don't know you, but I do. I have watched you grow, and as you have grown so have I. At first I didn't understand why me? But I knew whether Heaven or Earth you needed me as much as I needed you."

It was touching, and in that moment I couldn't shield myself from the heartache I was feeling. "But I am a horrible man."

He only smiles. Only someone who truly cares for you can smile this way. "You were a decent man, but all humans have flaws Jacob, including you."

I dry my eyes, and the evenings I spent in this glorious movie theater come back to me. The stone pillars, the balcony, the uncomfortable seats, the sticky floors, and the smell of stale popcorn. James turns to me and asks, "Do you want some?" I look at him puzzled, and he

disappears only for a moment. He arrives with popcorn and a
tall soda. I ask, "What is this?"

"Cherry Pepsi and popcorn," he responds.

Gabby and Danny's favorite. Tears that I had forced to
stop come spilling out again. My eyes are flowing like a
river, and the only one to blame is myself for my broken
heart.

Corinthians 4:8-9

"We are troubled on every side, yet not distressed; We are perplexed, but not in despair; Persecuted, but not forsaken; Cast down, but not destroyed."

Chapter 4: Gabby

Jake:

Absentee. Deadbeat. If there is an adjective for bad parenting, believe me it would perfectly describe my performance. I was around for my daughter until she was eleven. After Danny left, and took her it gave me my reason to disappear.

My will to succeed, my lust for life all evaporated, and I turned into the man I never wanted to be. I became a man with no family, no job, and a serious drinking problem.

As I sit comfortably in the Buckeye Theater, I guess an oxymoron considering the bad seating, I realize James nor I have spoken a word for quite some time. I recalled that earlier James had spoke of Gabby. So I turned to him and asked, "What do you know about my daughter?"

"Well, you have been dead about three years, so I have been watching over her for you," James replied.

"Three years?" I said, shocked and wondering where the time had gone.

"Yes, that is how long it takes the council of angels to decide."

"Decide? Decide on what?" I said.

"Yes, decide if you are more fit for Heaven or Hell," James retorted.

My mouth could only hang open as the shock of being dead three years set in. "It only felt like five minutes right?" James said with laughter in his voice trying to lighten my anxiety.

"What is hell like?" I asked curious, but without the will to find out for myself.

James gave me an answer, an honest answer, "I don't know I've never been."

Caught off guard by his response, because I assumed he knew all we both laughed, and something in this shared laughter felt right, safe, and loving.

When the laughter stopped I again asked the question that had been plaguing my mind since I arrived. "How's Gabby?"

James only nodded, and pointed toward the screen. And in that moment the lights dimed in the historic Buckeye Theater, and the screen began to flicker. What I saw next was the face of an angel. It was Gabby, James told me she was 38, but she looked worn and tired. Weathered from stress I assumed, but she is still as beautiful as I remember.

She was sitting alone in a study, becoming a better lawyer than I no doubt. She had long brown hair like her mother, but curly like mine use to be. She had deep brown eyes, and caramel skin, beautiful caramel skin like the tone of someone native to Mexico or Spain. I can recall the many boys I use to have to turn away, telling them "No! Gabrielle cannot come out to play!"

But what was she doing now? Why did she look so tired? Why was she so sad? What happened? James interrupted my thoughts, once again, and told me that Gabby was never the same after I killed myself. She had constantly been drinking, neglecting her husband, kids and work. I suppose in this instance the old saying "the apple doesn't far from the tree," is applicable.

James went on to tell me that she had been drinking for three years. I could just make out James's face in the glow of the screen, and the look resting upon it was compassionate yet it still seemed as if more bad news was on the horizon. He tried to smile, but he could only manage half, and it seemed to say brace yourself.

James cleared his throat, and began "About three years ago Gabby was pregnant with twins. Her husband Gordon and their two kids, Julian and Mason, were excited for the new arrivals. She was about seven months along when she found out you had killed yourself. She became extremely depressed."

I interrupted "are you trying to blame me for her problems?"

"No," James retorted, "but I will say that as her father you had a duty, an obligation that you did not fulfill. And for that you should be sorry. May I continue?"

I nodded, slightly taken back by the stern manner in which James had spoken to me. He reminded me so much of myself. Quick tempered, but gentle all the same.

James went on, "Gabby became depressed, and began drinking." Already knowing what question I had brewing in my mind James said, "yes, at seven months pregnant. She drank so much it forced her into early labor."

"Early labor?" I said shocked by her negligence.

James tilted his head back and forth, and continued. "The massive consumption of alcohol did things that were beyond repair. Gabby drank so much that it damaged the internal organs of the premature babies. Two months early, and alcohol ridden, the children did not stand a chance. Soon after Gordon left her and took the kids, and Gabby only drink harder, and slipped further and further. She lost her job as a prominent attorney, and here she sits."

James pointed at the screen, and I saw Gabby's tears steadily flowing from her eyes and a glass in her left hand and a bottle in her right. I was almost proud that her drink of choice was whiskey. For it had gotten me through many tough days, evenings, nights, hell who am I kidding it got me through everything. I watched Gabby as she sipped, and refilled her glass when it was half full. James then turned to me, and told me to listen. I could then hear Gabby's thoughts.

Gabby:

Here I sit, tired, sad, and nearing the end. Is this what I expected to be doing in my thirties? No family, no children, no husband and no father.

Oh my God! My babies! Tears are now falling down my face, and I can't stop them nor do I wish to. I don't deserve to live, and who knew in three years you could lose so much? I haven't spoken to my children since Gordon took them away from me. It is probably better this way?

I guess like father like daughter. Right Dad? That's all us Stevens are good for procreating then leaving.

I have buried my father, my babies, and now my hopes of ever leading a normal life. As I gaze at the ceiling I see a one-way ticket to whatever is next after this hell on Earth.

I sit on this uncomfortable wooden chair, which was given to Gordon and I in a dining room set as a wedding present from his parents, and I think what a waste I am. I never traveled the world. I won't see my children grow up, and I assume Gordon will remarry. The children's new mommy will replace me and I will be forgotten the same way my father forgot me. Sadly I can think of a million reasons to live, but only one to die.

Jake:

I watch my daughter cry her eyes out, and I can only be mortified at the decision I made. How selfish I was. She hadn't forgotten me, I had forgotten myself. How awful I was to her. Oh God what did I do? How could I have been a man to neglect my family? I can't bear to hear the sound of my Gabby's tears fall from her eyes. And just as I begin to lower my head in shame, I hear my daughter's thoughts again.

Gabby:

I remember my graduation day. Mom and Ron were so excited. But I had butterflies in my stomach, because of other reasons. I was almost certain Gordon was going to propose to me that evening. He was horrible at keeping secrets, and he had been constantly asking me if were still going out that night. My dear sweet Gordon, how I have failed you and the children with what have I become.

Gordon a tall man about 6'2 190 pounds, and a gorgeous smile, all the girls wanted him. Captain of the basketball team, double major, and involved in so many activities it use to make my head spin.

I was especially nervous; because I was so certain that my father was going to show up that day. Ron, Mom's new husband was okay but I could never take to him knowing he was not my father. He owned a furniture store, and all he ever talked about was just that, furniture. He had two kids of his own, Allison and Randy and I didn't particularly care for them much. They were 15 and 16 at the time, lived with their mother, and they were spoiled rotten.

I was so certain I was going to see Jake that I took extra long to get ready. I took so much time that mom said if I didn't hurry I would miss my own graduation. So I rushed knowing that the meaning of this day made my presence pertinent.

I wore a blue and yellow sundress, because it was warm but breezy. These gorgeous white sandals Mom had bought me, and I wore my hair down. Curly, but not too curly I didn't want to over do it.

The procession was like every graduation I had seen on T.V. crying, clapping, caps thrown, all of that typical stuff. Afterward I saw my whole family, and it was glorious. Grandma and Grandpa Hanson Mom's parents, cousins, aunts and uncles. They were all there to support me except one person or so I thought.

I congratulated friends, but something was still missing. I gave Gordon a kiss just as I was getting ready to go gather my things and head out with Mom and Ron. They had a special dinner planned with the whole family, and Gordon couldn't come until later due to the fact that his family was there as well. So we kissed and parted ways, and I immediately saw a man approaching me. At once I knew who it was. It was as if I had seen a ghost. "It's him, Jake," I remember saying to myself. Jake his name left a bitter taste in my mouth, so much to the point that I refuse to speak it, or even worse call him "Dad." Dad is a term used for men who are participants in their children's lives, and this was something Jake was not.

His face was the same as I remembered, identical to mine. But he seemed thinner, tired and worn down. They say God makes a daughter look like their father so the father won't leave them, but I guess this time it wasn't the case. I hadn't seen him since I was eleven. I hadn't really wanted to either, but I still had so much to say, so many questions to ask. Was I that bad of a daughter? What could I have done to make things better? Is it my fault? Why did you hate me? My Mother answered all of these questions, and she always said he loved me but things were just different for him. Although the answer is somewhat vague I gave in and I always tried to move on.

As Jake approached me all the things I wanted to say vanished. So there I stood with a blank mind, looking into the eyes of the man I hadn't seen in twenty plus years. When we were finally face to face all I could say to him was "Do I know you?" I could see the hurt in his eyes. I wanted to say sorry, but the involuntary movements of breathing and blinking were the only actions I could muster. He was a man crushed, dealt the final blow along the long tough road of life.

I felt a sort of payback or retribution, because for all these years this man had continuously broken my heart and I finally had my chance and I delivered. A daughter needs her father, but I guess he couldn't see it was me he was hurting in the end.

I could never trust men, and that was part of the problem with Gordon and I. I would always accuse him of lying and cheating, but I knew he never was. He loved me and only me. My father ruined me, and for that I will always hate him.

Jake:

How could I...? How was I...? I thought I was only punishing myself by staying away. How could I...? How was I...? Questions I couldn't answer nor could I finish. It's unfortunate when you grow into the man you want to be then one day you can do nothing as it all slips away. I am sobbing, taking pity upon myself for being an idiot. I can't control myself, and now I am yelling at the screen. "Gabby I am sorry! So, so sorry! Please forgive me! Don't do it, it's not worth it. What about your children? No...God...Please...Please God no!" I plead with God hoping that somehow, someway he will direct his grace upon her, and keep her from making the biggest mistake of her life.

James places his hand on my shoulder as if to tell me everything is okay. I can't hold back my tears. This is not at all what I thought Heaven would be, the non-stop crying and all this bad news. Once I dry my tears I go back to

listening to Gabby.

Ephesians 6:4

"Fathers, do not embitter your children, or they will become discouraged."

Chapter 5: Letter From A Father

Gabby:

I can remember when I was young, and I would go on picnics with Mom and Jake. I recall when I was about nine we went to the park. It was a really nice day, and we were having fun. I can remember Jake drinking, like he did so often. I thought it was cider, and now I know I was wrong. I wonder if alcoholism is hereditary? Ha! That's funny to think.

I remember he was drinking so much, and he got angry then began to scream. What he was upset about I do not recall, but he was clearly unhappy. Jake he just… he just snapped. He hit my mother in the face, and whether he punched or slapped her I do not remember. Mom fell to the ground and cried, and Jake he just left us. Left us at the park, and at nine I was left to pick up the pieces of his mistake. Much like I had to when I was eleven.

After Mom had to leave Jake things were not the same for a while, or ever for that matter. As I sit here and thumb the envelope that holds my fathers, or Jake's suicide letter, I consider reading it one last time. He writes as if he cares, as if he loves me, adores me, when his actions over the years said the opposite. As I position my fingers and open the envelope, with my other hand I pull out the letter. The paper is almost transparent, and I can see the dark ink on the other side. The paper is wrinkled, stained with my tears and my fathers to make out which stains belong to who is much like finding a needle in a haystack. I open the letter and begin to read the words.

Dearest Gabby:

I'm sorry… I know it's not enough. In fact there are not enough I'm sorrys to make it up to you. I wish the circumstances for you receiving this letter were different. I always envisioned myself as a father at ball games, or dance recitals, eventually giving you away at your wedding. I missed all of it, and everything in between. I never met your first date, or held you after your first broken heart. I am a failure. I am a failure as a man and father. I don't know when I reverted from a man to a boy, but I see now that transition was easy and my fatal mistake.

I wish I could erase the fact that I was a horrible parent, and held a position of no significance in your life. There are a myriad of things for me to apologize for, and to list them all would make things harder than they already are. I want you to know I am proud of you. I want you to know I cried at every milestone, and that was

because with each passing moment I became more and more
proud of you. I am sorry for not being your father, and for
being just a donor.

Tell your mother I am sorry for the hurt, and the
misery I put her through. I am sorry for putting my hands
on her, lying, cheating, and never listening to her when
she needed me most. I was supposed to be her rock, and just
as I let you down I did the same to her. She loved me
despite my faults, and to find the love of a good woman is
difficult. I still dream of your mother, but I dream more
about you. What your laugh must be like. What makes you
smile, and what makes you happy.

I took myself out of the equation, and I am sorry. I
love you, and whether my final words are written or spoken,
Gabrielle Christine Stevens I want you to know that I will
forever and always love you. You are my pride, my glory,
and my heart and soul. Never lose your spirit and always
keep a good head on your shoulders. Your mother is always
right so listen to her. I know you have a good man, so hold
on to him and never let go. Love Life! Every Moment! I Love
You!

DAD

Jake:

I watch my daughter as she finishes the letter that I had composed for her on my last day on Earth. I wonder if I was selfish? Should I have...? Was it too soon? I don't know what hurts more sitting here and watching tears stream endlessly down Gabby's face or the fact that I can't stop them from falling? I contemplate does Danny miss me the way I miss her? Does she think of me?

As my mind races I try to slow my breathing, and hope that settles me a bit. What is my problem? Why did I let them go? Had I known things would have turned out this way, I never would have done the things I did. I never would have said those things. I would have said sorry more, I would have loved more. The thing that I will most regret is letting go of the love of a good woman, and falling short in the eyes of my child.

Psalms 118:14

"The Lord is my strength and my song; he has become my salvation."

Chapter 6: A Mother's Sorrow

As I finish reading my father's letter for the final time I dream what he must have been thinking when he composed his final words. How did he feel? Did he really think he would go through with it? I sometimes wonder is it harder to live or to die? I think with life we become the person we want to be, but in death we will find out who we truly are.

Is there a God? How will he judge me? How will she look? Is God a man or a woman? Questions I remind myself will be answered in due time.

As I thumb the letter for the final time I watch as my tears soak the ink my father carefully placed between each line on the notebook paper. I place his letter back in the envelope. 2:30 p.m., time slowly passes when you know these are your final moments.

I take one last sip of the whiskey as if to say "goodbye old friend." I step up on the chair. The tears now flowing uncontrollably, and I fix the noose tightly around my neck. The noose is an old belt from the closet, new enough not to break, and sturdy enough to do the job. I brace myself for what is to come, but you can't prepare yourself for the end, can you? Am I selfish? Will people hate me? When no one loves you, no one can hate you. As I

feel the belt tighten around my neck, I look around the
dimly lit apartment. No memories, no family, no nothing,
only a lonely old hag soon to be dangling from the ceiling.

I kick the chair out from under me. Ahh it's tight. My
head is burning. Ears ringing. What did I do? I try to yell
help but I can't, and who would hear me anyway? God for
once help me! I've made a mistake! I don't want this! My
babies, Julian and Mason, mommy is so sorry. Lord please
let me take back this mistake. Not now. My head is burning;
it feels like my eyes are going to pop out of my head.
Someone save me, God for once someone help me! I can't go,
don't take me. My breath is shortening. I can't find air.
Is this how it ends? My air is gone, and my head burns less
and everything goes black.

I wake to crying. I can't make out faces, but there is
crying. I work harder to see, but the faces are
undecipherable. My vision clears, and I see my mother and
my two boys crying. I try to speak, and nothing comes out.
I'm lying down. Where am I? Someone help! Where am I? Mom!
Mom! Help me! I'm sorry. I didn't mean to! Lord let me go
back to my babies! I'm sorry! I'm Sorry!

To my Darling Children Julian and Mason:

All I can say is I am sorry. You two should already know what has happened to me, but you won't know the reason why I did it until you finish this letter. I have regressed into a person who I can't even recognize. I was once a happy mother and a loving wife, but somewhere along the road that all changed. The death of my father did something to me that all the words in the world couldn't do justice, and it was not for the better. I know you both know that I took that very hard, but I want you to know that what has happened now is not because of you.

It's because I am weak, worthless, and a horrible mother. I have failed in all aspects of my life. Please forgive me. You two will grow to be big strong men, and you will realize that there is more to life than material items. You two I'm sure will marry, and have children of your own. Love your families; keep them close and never let go. I should have done that, but I didn't. Please learn from my mistakes.

Your Daddy I am assuming with remarry, love his wife with all your hearts. She is the closet thing you will have to a mother. I was never much of one, but for that I am sorry. Just promise me that everyday you will Love Life! Cherish Every Moment! And Be Happy! If you do those three

things you will live fulfilling lives. I will always love
you!

      Mommy

St. Luke 17:3

"Take heed to yourselves: If thy brother trespass against thee, rebuke him; and if he repent, forgive him."

Chapter 7: Hello Again

The theater screen goes black, and the lights come back on. I turn and look at my brother, and my eyes are full of tears. James turns his head slightly, and smiles. He gives me a look as if to say, "everything is going to be okay." I can only muster half of the gesture that he gives me.

I turn back to the screen, and I want to ask what happens next to Gabby. But instead I say nothing. James places his hand on my shoulder, and only says "She is on her way home now." I understand, but I don't want to understand. I can only place my head in my hands and cry. I want to ask James "why all the pain? Why all the heartache? If this is heaven why does it hurt so bad? What if Gabby doesn't make it here?"

Like a brother that has spent his entire life with me, he takes me in the nook of his arm and says "brother it's not for us to understand. There is a plan. One that you and I may not want, but it's his plan."

James goes on to tell me that there is someone who wants to see me. He grabs me by the hand and tells me to close my eyes. I do as he says never once flinching at the gentle and loving touch of a brother I've never known, but have always known. I close my eyes, and I feel peace but only for a moment.

James then tells me to open my eyes. I am standing in the most beautiful garden. Stargazer lilies, white roses, shrubs, trees, a pond, the beauty is endless. Since I have arrived in heaven this is the second most beautiful thing I have seen. Here there seems to be no pain, no heartache, and no worries. I take my hand from James's, and I turn in circles to take it all in. As I am looking off into the distance I ask James "where are we?" I get no response, and when I turn around he is no longer there. After he has long disappeared I shout, "Is God a man or woman?" No answer.

Alone I stand in this garden of flowers. Alone, the theme to my life, and now my after life. I am alone or so I think until I hear the quite soft voice of a man. "Jake… Jake…"

I turn, and there I stand face to face with my father. "How long… how lo…"

"How long has it been?" My father finishes my sentence. Norman Stevens. The strong silent type, not too tall maybe about 5'9, but had the voice of a giant. A stern man, with the gentle side like that of a child. Always willing to give, but would hand down punishment when it was deserved. He was never fat, but he was always pleasantly round. I learned growing up that my father was a man of little words, but his actions spoke louder than anything he could have said. I learned the ways of the world through the eyes of my father. My manners, my whit, and charm all came from him. I am truly my father's child.

As I look my father in his eyes I can only think of the last time I saw him. At that point I was 22 years old, and I was running off with Danielle to get married. She had gotten pregnant with Gabby, and we had known we were in love. Gabby only gave us a better reason to runaway together. I can remember the hurt and disappointment in his eyes when I told him I was to marry Danielle. He told me that since I had graduated from college, and was paying my own bills I could make any decision I deemed necessary. He went on to say that he didn't agree with what I was doing, but he could respect it. I had approached him and told him like a man. He had never been a fan of Danny, and not too many people were. They didn't see what I saw. Her long brown hair, which complemented her heavenly round face, a voice yet whiney at times, could have been confused for that of an angel.

I remember that was the last time I had spoken to my father. He never called, wrote, or showed up for a visit but I guess I can't really blame him because neither did I.

He had written me off for the decision I made. He never
actually said it, but I knew that was the reason we hadn't
spoken. After I stopped talking to my father I banished
myself from my family, except Danielle and Gabby. They were
all I needed, or so I thought until Danny left me. After
that I needed my family, but by then I was so far gone
there was nothing I could do.

My father looked me in the eyes, and smiled. I could
only stare. He said it has been over ten years since we had
seen each other. I wanted to say sorry, but was I really
sorry? I had missed him. Thought of him. I wanted to go to
his funeral, but I didn't have the nerve. I cried for
months. Was I sorry? I was sorry for the way our
relationship ended, but not sorry for being with Danny. And
if he thought I was going to apologize for that he was
sadly mistaken.

He placed his hand on mine, and said in a knowing tone
"son, you are preparing yourself for an argument that isn't
going to take place. I know you are sorry, and so am I. We
can't change the past, but what we can do is move forward
and build a relationship from this point onward. I want you
to know I am proud of you, and I always have been and I
always will be. Where we went wrong long ago, was my lack
of consideration for your feelings and your stubborn

attitude. Had I understood the love that you shared for Danielle then maybe things would have been different? But I now know that your relationship with her wasn't for me to understand. I wanted you to be happy, and I am glad you got to share happiness with someone whom you love."

I could only bow my head, and cry tears of shame and happiness. There in a garden in Heaven, Norman Stevens father, and Jake Stevens son hugged for the first time in over a decade.

My father and I talked for what seemed like hours. Everything I had been through from the divorce to committing suicide. He told me that things get tough, but it wasn't my responsibility to take away something that was generously bestowed upon me.

"Life is a gift" he said, "The most blessed gift in the world, what you did was take your life for granted Jake. You didn't realize there were people depending on you, Gabrielle mostly. You let your life get away from you, that happens to the best of us. But what makes us who we are is how we recover from the bad times. It's easy to be happy when everything is going our way, but who are we when the shit hits the fan?"

"But…" my father stopped me from speaking.

"But nothing son! You had it all Danielle, Gabrielle, a good job. What more could you have asked for? A good woman, a beautiful daughter, you let it go."

"Is heaven here to make you dwell on your mistakes? Why am I here?" I asked him.

My father gave me the look that could stop the most cold hearted individual in their tracks. I remember this look from my childhood, and the last time I remember being on the receiving end was when Danielle and I ran away together. It was a look of anger and disappointment.

"Heaven isn't here to make you dwell on your mistakes son. Heaven is here to make you put your life into perspective. Help you see what you did wrong, and to help you see what makes humans, humans. God loves us unconditionally, and Heaven shows us that even in the darkest of hours there is always someone watching over us. Just as James and I did for you."

"If you were watching over me then why didn't you stop me from, from…"

"From what?" my father said.

"From killing myself? Why did you let me slip to the point that I did? Why didn't you reach out to me? Tell me I was foolish? Why did you let Danny leave me? Why did you let me grow so far from Gabby? If God truly loves me why didn't he help me? If he truly cared why was my life such a disaster? You know who loves me? No one! That's why I am here. I am better off in hell!" As I said this I tried to turn away from my father, but he placed his hand upon my shoulder firmly.

My father then bowed his head, and in a low muffled tone said "You don't mean any of that. Son you are here because you have a good heart. Everyone is given choices it's what you do with those choices that determines the outcome of your life. God isn't spiteful; he isn't a vengeful God, he only wishes you would walk in the light of the Holy Spirit. You lost your way son, that's all." My father then smiled a smile that only a father could.

I sat there; upset blaming everyone else for my mistakes when I should have realized long ago my mistakes were just that, my mistakes.

My father released my shoulder, "Jake I have to go now, but I will see you again. You have other things you must see. Remember Heaven is a place of learning and eternal happiness. At this point it seems as if happiness will never come, but you have to let go in order to let new things come in. You will understand."

And with that my father was gone. I reached out to touch him, but nothing was there. I didn't notice the tears

falling from my eyes until I licked my lips and tasted the
saltiness that only tears could provide. I wondered what
else I would see. Was it Gabby? Where is Gabby? Why isn't
she here yet? I thought…? I sat down next to a large stone
in the water, and looked upward toward what I imagine was
the sky. The sun shined brightly, and birds chirped. I
slowly drifted off to sleep, and felt peace a feeling I
calmly welcomed.

James 5:16

"Confess your faults one to another, and pray one for another, that ye may be healed…"

Chapter 8: Hello

Gabby:

"Ha-ha… Ha-ha"… I hear laughter, but what is it? My eyes are heavy, and I am tired but I feel so peaceful. I am trying to open my eyes, but the light is too bright. Where am I? Am I dead? Oh God! Am I dead? Is this a hospital? I try and open my eyes again, but that light is too bright. What is going on? "Hahaha… Hahaha… Mommy watch! Mommy wake up! Mommy! Mommy!"

Who is that? Whose voices are those? Are they talking to me? I finally bear the light, and open my eyes. I am lying on a park bench. There are two boys playing on the swing set at the park. Twin boys. Twin… Twin… Twin boys. "Mommy look!"

'Mommy?' Who me? I have never seen these children before.

One of the boys hops off the swing set and is now running toward me. "Mommy, Mommy!" He looks about four years old. But why are they calling me mommy? "Who are you?" I ask. He smiles and takes me by the hand. The other boy runs over and takes the other one. Hand in hand with two children I have never met before, they are dragging me to an unknown destination. I guess I should be more apprehensive, but I am curious. As they are dragging me along, I ask them questions. "Where are your parents? Who are you? Where am I?" All of which go unanswered. They simply look at each other after each question and giggle as if they have all the information, but are playing a game not to give it to me. After about five minutes or so of being dragged along by two random children I begin to get agitated.

I come to a stop, and tell the boys enough is enough who are you? The boy to my right his eyes begin to fill with tears. He pauses for a moment and says, "You don't remember us do you?"

I shake my head.

The other one says "Mommy it's us. Remember? The two you... you... you know..."

I'm confused. "The two I what? The two I what? What is going on here?" I say becoming more and more angry with each passing moment.

The little boy on the right with tears in his eyes says "it's us mom. Your twin boys who you... you... killed."

My eyes widen and I start to shake my head. I am backing up now. "No" I say "No, no but you're, you're dead." My words are hollow. Tears are falling from my eyes. "Where am I? Who are you? This isn't funny."

The one on the left, he seems to be the stronger of the two say, "It's okay mommy, we won't hurt you. You hurt us but we forgive you. God brought us home. We have been waiting for you."

"But how? How? What are you names?"

The boy on the right has stopped crying and says with a smile "I'm Ethan!"

I only have a moment to marvel at how quickly the boys emotions change. "Ethan" I say under my breath.

"That's Ethan" the boy on the left says, "And I'm Alex", and as if it were all normal Ethan then tackles Alex and they being to tumble around, laughing and giggling.

I wait for them to finish rough housing, and I ask them where I am.

Ethan looks at me as if I asked the world's dumbest question, and says "you're in heaven silly. We came here after we didn't make it to be with you Mommy."

Alex chimes in "yeah, and it's so much fun. We have so many friends, and my favorite food is Mac and Cheese."

I can only giggle to myself. These boys, so precious, so pure, so loving, and I took their lives. I took their lives through stupidity. I was selfish. How could I? How could I be…?

Alex places his hand on mine, and says "Mommy don't blame yourself. You were sad. We aren't mad at you, we love you."

The tears begin to flow like old habit. It's just like riding a bike. Alex wraps his arms around me, and Ethan does the same. I was horrible to them yet they still love me. What did I do to deserve such good children? As they hold me tightly I'm dumbfounded with the capacity of forgiveness within a child's heart.

As I stop crying Alex tells me that it is not them who I am there to see. I ask them who, but they don't tell me. They just tell me to follow them. As we walk along the path Alex and Ethan ask about their father and their older brother's Julian and Mason. I tell them how Julian is the artistic one, and Mason is the athlete. I go on and on about Julian's painting and piano playing and how I hope that one day he goes to a prestigious art school to pursue his dreams. I go into how Mason is an amazing basketball player, and how I hope he plays division one and achieves his dreams of the NBA.

I talk for what seems like hours, and in the distance I see a figure. A tall figure, I can't make out the face but something about it seems so familiar. As I get closer, and closer I begin to realize who it is… Jake.

As I see Jake approaching I try to tighten the grip on Alex and Ethan's hands but my hands are empty. I look to my left and my right, but no one is there. Alone I stand as I wait for the man who I have longed to spend time with since I was eleven.

As I make my way closer to Jake, my father, I feel old feelings of hatred and resentment rush back to me. It is a flood of emotions, a flood that I have not prepared a dam to stop.

Does he recognize me? Will he speak to me? I tell myself to turn around, but it is as if my feet are stuck in cement. I try to say something, but I can conjure no words. All I can do is watch as Jake inches closer and closer. With each breath I take it feels like a lifetime, each footstep he takes seems to be slow and methodical. I realize there is no turning back now, because we are face to face. He smiles. And this is the beginning of the first real conversation I have had with my father since I was eleven.

1 Peter 4:8

"Above all, love each other deeply, because love covers over a multitude of sins."

Chapter 9: The Last Dance

"How are you?" Jake says, almost hesitant and you can tell these are the only words he can find to start the conversation.

"Fine" I say, "and you?"

He pauses for a moment, and in this instant I was able to take the time out to realize what he is wearing. A white gown, glowing almost, he seems somewhat heavenly. Very different from the dark drunken father that I have known from my past.

After the pause that seemed to hold us both in place, my father responded "Dead!" but with a smile. This was the first time I had shared a laugh with this man. Uncomfortable yes, but it felt right. I got the feeling that the dust was slowly being swept away from our relationship, and it was almost time for a new beginning. But I had so many questions, and I need so many answers.

After the smiles had long gone from our faces I finally had the courage to ask the questions I have been dying to ask for years. "Why did you leave us? Why did you leave me? I am your daughter. How could you?"

Jake cut me off. He spoke softly, with a regretful tone, a tone of sorrow and guilt. "I don't know why. Things became too hard. The alcohol too much. How could I be a good father when I was struggling to be a good man? I was worthless I didn't deserve you or your mother. I should have killed myself a long time ago. I wish I could have saved you from all the hurt and pain I have caused you, but here you are and here I am. I failed you as a father and I understand that. You don't have to forgive me, but I hope you will and I pray that we can start new. Gabby I truly am sorry."

When Jake finished, I could only turn my head to the distance. I tried to conceal my anger, my hurt, and the disbelief that even after all this time I still loved him unconditionally. But my attempts were futile, because the tears I tried to hide began to fall from my eyes.

When I composed myself enough to speak, I spoke with hurt and anger in my voice. "I haven't really seen you since I was eleven, and the last time I did see you was my college graduation. I know you use to send letters to Mom from time to time to see how I was doing, but why couldn't you write me? What did I do that was so wrong? How could you walk out on us? You were a horrible father, and I turned into you. It's your fault! I wouldn't be, I wouldn't be… Oh God! I wouldn't be dead if it weren't for you."

Jake put his arms around me, I felt uncomfortable but only for a moment and I knew this is where I always belonged, in the arms of my father.

Jake began to speak and it sounded as if all the hurt and disappointment he had given out over the years were lodged in his throat, "Gabrielle Christine, my claim was never that I was the best father and I have never claimed to be a good man. But there is one thing that I know for sure, and that is I am sorry from the bottom of my heart for the way things have turned out. I was not there for you, when you graduated high school, college, law school, I didn't even give you away at your wedding." Jake then pulled away from me releasing me from his embrace and lowered his head, and in this moment I no longer looked at him as a stranger but I saw him as my father. A father that had made mistakes, a father that if given the opportunity would do things differently. I guess sometimes life deals you cards, and it's up to you to play the right hand.

With his head lowered my father spoke again, "I tried to keep going for you, but in the end I felt I should give up for you. I gave up on me so you wouldn't have to see me as the failure I had become. My biggest fear was you coming to me, and asking me why I was never around and I knew I would never have the right answer or even a good answer. My life became a downward spiral, and I just didn't know how to save myself. I brought all of those bad things on, and I wish I could go back and change it but unfortunately I cannot. Gabby I don't know how many times I am going to say this or how many times I need to say this but I am truly sorry. If you give me the opportunity I promise I can make up for lost time."

I then began to speak, and the words flowed from me like music. "Dad, I have hated you, loved you, hated you, and loved you it is really an endless cycle. I am tired of hurting. I needed you, and where were you? Where were you when I was giving up on me? Why? When I looped that belt around my neck why didn't you tell me to stop? You are supposed to protect me. I'm not mad at you, you are weak and for that I am sorry."

"Gabrielle, I can't be to blame for all your problems. Some of that goes on you, but what I can be to blame for is not being the father you deserved. I agree I am weak, but honey I am sorry to say you are just as weak as I. You gave up. I wish I could have held your hand when you were sad, kissed your forehead and told you 'everything is going to be okay,' but I wasn't there and all I can say is I am sorry."

"Dad, I am scared. I am scared to lose you again. I don't want to love you and get use to having you in my life or my heavenly existence and have you go away. Heaven is supposed to be a place of happiness, but why am I so scared?"

"Honey, Heaven is the place where you confront all of your deepest darkest secrets. It's not meant to hurt you it is here to open your eyes. Give you peace after death. Once you have confronted all the secrets, all the fears and anxieties you can then bask in the light of the God. Gabby, God has brought us together for a reason, and I don't think he is going to let us separate again. You deserve my love and I deserve yours so there is nothing to be afraid of just let Heaven do its work."

Dad and I then began to walk down a paved path. Birds were chirping, and all seemed to be right. We reminisced about times from my childhood, and I told him about my life after he left and he told me of his. I felt this was the way things were supposed to be, but they hadn't been like this for years.

Along the path my father stopped and picked a beautiful lily and placed it in my hair. I knew that if I tried to speak in that moment the only thing to come out would be a tear.

All that was missing was Mom, and Dad definitely agreed. Dad hoped he would be part of my mother's heaven, and in the words he spoke at that moment I truly realized how deeply he cared for her.

"Gabby, your mother was an angel that I didn't deserve. Did we have our troubles? Yes, but so does everyone else. I knew her and she knew me. We were like two lost souls that became one when we found one another. I know it's cheesy, but she was everything I had been looking for and more. Your mother and I developed a kind of trust and relationship that it takes people years to develop. It only took us 3 years, and it was in those three years that I knew I had found my soul mate and to keep looking was pointless. So we got married young, I was 22 and she was 23. We then had you, and you were the icing to an already perfect cake. We were a perfect family, but all of that changed. I messed it up Gabby, I messed it up for you and your mother. When she left me I'm not truly sure how I kept going. I think I was just numb to it all, maybe hoping she would come back to me, I don't really know? I have hurt many people in my life Gabby, but hurting you two was the biggest regret I ever had. Even Heaven can't remove the guilt that has riddled my heart."

I smiled, and took his hand. I took my right hand while tightly clutching his right hand with my left hand, and I wiped the tears falling from his eyes. He looked old and tired, and as I examined his face we began to hear music in the distance. Both of us startled we turned and faced the direction it was coming from. It sounded lovely, and the music kissed the air with such grace and tenderness. I looked to my father and he had the same expression as I, the look that said, "shall we investigate?"

As we walked along the paved path looking for the destination in which the music had come from, it began to get louder and louder and we could hear the voices of people in the distance.

We came to a small hill, and once we cleared it we saw a beautiful sight, a large tent with hundreds of people under it laughing, joking and having a good time. As we came down the hill the music stopped and everyone turned toward us. Father and daughter, arm in arm, smiling from ear to ear. Both dressed in white gowns as if we had risen from bed, but never decided to change. They all were dressed the same, but the funny thing about these gowns is there were no wrinkles and all of them seemed to give off a dim light.

When we got closer to the crowd a small elderly woman
emerged from the cluster of people. It was my Grandmother
Stevens, and the look on my father face was that of a man
who's past had just come back to haunt him.

Jake:

Gabrielle and I have been walking and talking along a
beautifully paved path lined with flowers. Not just any
flowers, but Danielle and Gabby's favorite flowers. There
were stargazer lilies, pink roses, red roses, white roses,
tulips, and I knew the lilies were Gabby's favorite amongst
them so I picked one and placed it in her hair. She smiled,
and I admired her for accepting me as her father and in
that moment I couldn't have been happier.

As we were walking we began to hear music. Beautiful
music that could have only been fit for the ears of angels.
We made our way up a hill to investigate, and as we came
over it we saw a huge white tent with tons of people. It
looked like a family reunion, people laughing and smiling.
Gabby and I were hesitant to make our way down, because we
did not want to interrupt this festive gathering. But when
we became visible to most of those in attendance the music
stopped and all at once the people faced us. It was as if

they had planned for us to come, as if they had been waiting wondering when we were to arrive.

We inched our way down the hill, and an elderly woman emerged from the crowd. She had the biggest smile on her face, and I could not understand why. As we neared I understood the smile, and I realized I was seeing a woman I hadn't seen or spoken to in years, my mother.

It was as if I had seen the ghost of the woman who had once called me her son, her sunshine, and everything that made her happy in this world. She always saw things in me that others couldn't. She always told me that I was to be great, but I never believed her. I bet she never thought I would end up like this. That I would end up in heaven, with what I was to assume was a guest past and that my delivery to hell would come in due time. I had taken life that she, my father, and God had graciously given me.

Was I selfish? This I am certain I was. Does she know why I am here? I am sure she does. Does she still love me? Does she know I didn't even go to her funeral? I didn't stop talking to her because I hated her, but it was because I was afraid she was disappointed. Who wouldn't be disappointed? You bear a child who you believe can turn the world upside down, but instead he turns his own world upside down. He becomes the bottom of the barrel, the worst. I want to hug her, and tell her I am sorry, sorry for everything. Sorry for everything I have become, sorry for not being there, sorry for being the mess up that I was and still am.

As I neared my mother, my heart began to break, tears had not began to fall from my eyes but she said to me "Son don't cry, please, please don't cry." All I could do was collapse, and Janine Stevens a 5'5 100 pound woman caught me. She caught me like she always had. Caught me when I had gotten my heartbroken in the 10th grade, caught me when I was sad I couldn't play outside when I had broken my leg when I fell from a tree, and now she caught me as my heart broke from disappointing my mother. I had been an estranged son for years, but the love of your mother is never lost.

She held me in her arms, swaying back and forth and she kept saying "lay it on me child." My mother always said this, whenever I was sad, hurt, angry, anything. She would always let me "lay my problems" on her. She was always there for me, and me, I was never there for her.

I don't know if Gabby or any of the others were watching, but in that moment I didn't care because I was in the arms of an angel.

Gabby:

For the first time I saw my father as a man. Crying, sobbing to the mother he had once grown apart from. I wondered what the others thought of this sight, and when I picked my head up to look at them, they all had tears in their eyes. They all knew that this was what family was all about. You can leave your family, but you can never leave their love.

Jake:

I picked myself up with the aid of my mother, and she put both of her hands on the sides of my face and looked at me and smiled. She spoke softly, "where have you been honey? We have been waiting for you."

I wanted to tell her everything, but the look in her eyes said she knew it all. All the hurt, Gabby, Danny, everything. She looked over my shoulder, and saw Gabby, and the sparkle that was in her eyes was that of a proud Grandmother. She walked around me, and embraced her granddaughter. She took us both by the hand, and led us into the party.

As we strolled through the gathering I greeted relatives I hadn't seen in years, uncles, aunts, cousins, all that had passed and some I had never known. I saw one aunt in particular that I lost when I was eleven, my aunt

Christine. She had always been like a mother to me, and she had lost her life in a fire at the young age of 32. I had waited my whole life to see her, and here she was. I ran to her like I was a child again, and embraced her. I never wanted to let go. I told her I loved her, and how I missed her, and how I wish I had been there to help her when the fire had started.

She told me it wasn't my fault and there was nothing I could do. She went on to say she was proud of me, and all that I had accomplished in my life, and that she had always checked in on me.

My Aunt and I grew very close, and as a small child I was attached to her hip like an appendage. She took care of me while my parents worked, and I did the same for her.

She had a serious case of multiple sclerosis, and I had watched it wreak havoc on her body. With each passing day, week, month I watched her get worse. I watched her move around her house in pain. While her husband was out living another life, my aunt struggled increasingly to do day-to-day activities. She was a strong woman who never complained, who never broke, and one who never waivered in her faith. She was strong; I can recall hoping that one day I would be half the person that she was.

I had always hoped that Gabby would end up with her strong will, and that is how Danielle and I had chosen Gabby's middle name. Gabrielle Christine Stevens.

To make it through her death I told myself that the God needed her, and that she was in a better place. A place where her legs worked again like they use to, she could run, laugh, smile, and watch over those who loved her most.

I released my lovely aunt from my grasp, kissed her on the cheek, and set out to find Gabby and my mother amongst the crowd of family. As I waded through my family members, I found them sitting at a table, hand in hand and smiling and laughing as if they never been apart. I paused for a moment, and let them be as I took a mental picture. Two generations of Stevens women. What could they be talking about? Children? Husbands? School? Life? I'm sure all of it.

Gabby:

As I see my father make his way to someone I have never met, my Grandmother and I make our way through the crowd periodically stopping to talk to relatives I didn't even know I had. There were tons of aunts, great aunts, uncles, great uncles, and cousins. They all seemed like

they were a tight knit group and I wondered if things had
always been like this?

Holding the hand of my Grandmother she led me to a
small empty table on the other side of the party. The view
from this table was like nothing I had ever seen before.
There was a large lake with many tents and gazebos lining
the shore. I imagined that there were other families who
were doing the same as we were, because I could hear the
music off in the distance.

My grandmother, and I talked about everything,
children, marriage, life, everything. If it could be a
topic it was covered. She spoke with such kindness, and in
her voice there was love with an undertone of knowledge and
wisdom. Her face was older, but beautiful nonetheless. Her
hands were wrinkled, but you could tell it was from hard
work. Her hair was gray, but it was from leading a
beautiful life and bearing beautiful children.

We never spoke of what I had done to my young boys, or
myself but I felt like she knew, but she loved me despite
my mistakes. As I sat there hand in hand with my
grandmother it felt like she had never gone. It felt like
she has always been with me. I am beginning to think Heaven
is about family, love and appreciating all that the Lord
has given us.

Jake:

As I stand there and watch Gabrielle and my mother, her grandmother, I feel a since of pride. In the background I hear the Electric Slide playing, a definite family reunion tradition, and I see all of my relatives doing the dance. One of my relatives grabs me, and I make my way to the dance floor, and I join them. Laughing, and smiling, this is a feeling I have not had the pleasure of partaking in years. As the song ends, I feel that I am sweating, not from over work, but from having too much fun. Just then I hear the first notes of my favorite song, Eric Clapton Tears in Heaven, and I rush to find Gabby at the table.

I see someone has gotten to her before I. She is hand in hand with a dance partner, my Uncle Ian. I kindly ask him if I can have this dance, and jokingly he takes my hand and says of course. We laugh and exchange a hug, and I take Gabrielle's hand and lead her to the dance floor.

We slowly walk to the middle, and all of our relatives part. I place my hand on her waist, and her hand on my shoulder, I take her left hand in my right and we begin to sway to the music. As we dance around we notice that the dance floor has emptied, and the tent is empty as well, we are the only two under what seems to be white Christmas lights. We don't mind, and our movements never miss a beat. We gaze into each other eyes, and begin to cry. She cries because she missed me, and I cry because I have missed her. I squeeze her tightly hoping this moment never ends. As the last of the songs melody hits the wind, I whisper into her ear "I am your father, I always have been, I always will be. My love for you will never change. I will cherish this time we have had together, and I hope Heaven permits us to have more. I will never stray from you again. You are my heart, my soul, and you mean everything to me. To you I am eternally grateful for giving me back the time I have missed. I love you Gabrielle Christine Stevens."

"What matters now will not matter 100 years from now. It will not matter what kind of car I drove, what kind of house I lived in, how much I had in my bank account, nor what my clothes looked like. But the world may be a little better because I was important in the life of a child."

-Unknown

DEDICATION

First and foremost I want to thank God. He has helped me become what I am today, and I am eternally grateful. I know I wouldn't have seen the things I have seen or done the things I have done without him. He has carried me through every tough situation, and I know I am still standing because of him.

There are two people who I wish to thank for being the kind of people who adults and children can look up to. The first is my older cousin Jessica. Jessee you work hard, and you deserve a day off, a month off, who am I kidding you deserve the whole year! You are super mom, and you honestly should get an award! I love you from the bottom of my heart, and I am proud to be in the same family as you.

Second is my older cousin E.J. You are the best dad in the world. You work outrageous hours, but still find time for your kids. I hope that one day I can be half the father to my daughter that you are to your kids. I have looked up to you since childhood, and I will continue to do so in my adult life. I love you.

Shout out to my entire family, my friends (Especially Alana Wilkinson), my lovely girlfriend Whitney and her family (Tori, Taylor, Christine, and Rob), Ruby Tuesday

Zanesville (Kayla Patts, Danielle, Molly, Lawrence, John, Dr. Uppole, Kelly, Joel, Brittany, Anne, Joanna, Courtney, Stash, Tone, Mark, Sam, Rick, man everybody there you know who you are), lastly New Concord, Ohio for molding me into the person I am today.